SHAKSPERE FO.

MACBETH

AS ABRIDGED BY

CHARLES KEMBLE,

WITH

NOTES FOR SCHOOL USE.

LONDON: GEORGE BELL AND SONS, YORK STREET,

COVENT GARDEN.

1883.

PERSONS REPRESENTED.

DUNCAN, King *of* Scotland.
MALCOLM,
DONALBAIN, } *his Sons.*
MACBETH,
BANQUO, } *Generals of the* King's Army.
MACDUFF,
LENOX, } *Noblemen of* Scotland.
ROSSE,
FLEANCE, *Son to* Banquo.
SIWARD, *General of the English Forces.*
SEYTON, *an* Officer *attending on* Macbeth.
A Doctor.
A Soldier.

Lady MACBETH.
Gentlewoman *attending on* Lady Macbeth.
Hecate, and three Witches.

    Lords, Gentlemen, Officers, Soldiers, *and* Attendants.

SCENE, *in the end of the Fourth Act, lies in* England ;
through the rest of the play, in Scotland ; *and, chiefly, at*
Macbeth's *Castle.*

————

NOTE.—The following version is reprinted from the copy
of Shakspere used by the late Charles Kemble in his public
readings. By its careful abridgment, by the omission of all
objectionable passages, and the occasional accentuation of
emphatic words, it is well adapted for school use, with a view
to which short notes have also been appended.

MACBETH.

ACT I.

An open Place.

Thunder and Lightning.   Enter three Witches.

1 *Witch.*

WHEN shall we three meet again
In thunder, lightning, and in rain?
   2 *Witch.* When the hurlyburly's done,
When the battle's lost and won.
   3 *Witch.* That will be ere the set of
sun.
  1 *Witch.* Where the place?
  2 *Witch.*   Upon the heath:
  3 *Witch.* There I go to meet Macbeth.
  All. Fair is foul, and foul is fair:
Hover through fog and filthy air.

                          [*Witches vanish.*

A Camp near Fores.

Alarum within. Enter King Duncan, Malcolm, Donalbain, Lenox, *with Attendants, meeting a bleeding* Soldier.

Duncan.

HAT bloody man is that? He can report,
As seemeth by his plight, of the revolt
The newest state.

Mal.   This is the sergeant, who
Like a right good and hardy soldier, fought
'Gainst my captivity:—Hail, hail, brave friend!
Say to the king the knowledge of the broil,
As thou didst leave it.

Sold.   Doubtful long it stood;
As two spent swimmers, that do cling together,
And choke their art.   The merciless Macdonel
Show'd like a rebel; but was all too weak;
For brave Macbeth (well he deserves that name),
Disdaining fortune, with his brandish'd steel,
Carv'd out his passage, till he fac'd the slave;
And fix'd his head upon our battlements.

Dun. O valiant cousin!

Sold.   King of Scotland, mark:
No sooner justice had, with valour arm'd,
Compell'd these skipping Kerns to trust their heels;
But the Norweyan lord, with new supplies,
Began a fresh assault.

Dun.   Dismay'd not this
Our captains, brave Macbeth and Banquo?

Sold.   Yes;
As sparrows, eagles; or the hare, the lion!
But I am faint, my gashes cry for help.

Dun. So well thy words become thee, as thy
   .wounds;
They smack of honour both.—But who comes here?
                    [*Exit Soldier attended.*

Enter ROSSE *and* ANGUS.

Mal. The worthy thane of Rosse.
Rosse.   ·   God save the king!
Dun. Whence cam'st thou, worthy thane?
   Rosse.   From Fife, great king;
Where the Norweyan banners flout the sky,
And fan our people cold.   Norway himself,
Assisted by that most disloyal traitor
The thane of Cawdor, 'gan a dismal conflict:
Point against point, rebellious arm 'gainst arm,
Curbing his lavish spirit.—To conclude,
The victory fell on us;——
   Dun.   Great happiness!
   Rosse. Now Sweno, Norway's king, craves com-
      position;
Nor would we deign him burial of his men,
Till he disbursed, at Saint Colmes' Isle,
Ten thousand dollars to our general use.
   Dun. No more that thane of Cawdor shall deceive
Our bosom's trust :—Pronounce his present death,
And with his former title greet Macbeth.   [*Exeunt.*

A Heath.

Thunder. Enter the three Witches.

1 *Witch.*

HERE hast thou been, sister?
    2 *Witch.* Killing swine.
    3 *Witch.* Sister, where thou?
  1 *Witch.* A sailor's wife had chestnuts in her lap,
And mounch'd, and mounch'd, and mounch'd :—
    Give me, quoth I :
Aroint thee, witch ! the rump-fed ronyon cries.
Her husband's to Aleppo gone, master o' the Tiger:
But in a sieve I'll thither sail,
And, like a rat without a tail,
I'll do, I'll do, and I'll do.
  2 *Witch.* I'll give thee a wind.
  3 *Witch.* And I another.
  1 *Witch.* I myself have all the other :
I will drain him dry as hay :
Sleep shall neither night nor day
Hang upon his pent-house lid ;
He shall live a man forbid :
Weary sev'n-nights nine times nine,
Shall he dwindle, peak, and pine.
Though his bark cannot be lost,
Yet it shall be tempest-toss'd.
Look what I have.
  2 *Witch.*   Show me, show me.
  1 *Witch.* Here I have a pilot's thùmb,
Wrack'd, as hòmeward he did come. [*Drum within.*
  3 *Witch.* A drum, a drum ; Macbeth doth come.
  All. The weird sisters, hand in hand,
Posters of the sea and land,

Thus do go about, about.
Thrice to thine, and thrice to mine,
And thrice again, to make up nine.

Enter MACBETH *and* BANQUO.

Macb. So foul and fair a day I have not seen.
Ban. How far is't call'd to Forres?—What are
    these,
So wither'd, and so wild in their attire;
That look not like the inhabitants o' the earth,
And yet are on't?—Live you? or are you aught
That man may question? You seem to understand me,
By each at once her choppy finger laying
Upon her skinny lips:—You should be wòmen,
And yet your beards forbid me to interpret
That you àre so.
    Macb.   Speak, if you can;—What are you?
   1 *Witch.* All hail, Macbeth! hail to thee, thane
    of Glamis!
   2 *Witch.* All hail, Macbeth! hail to thee, thane
    of Cawdor!
   3 *Witch.* All hail, Macbeth! that shalt be Kìng
    hereafter.
   Ban. Good sir, why do you start; and seem to fèar
Things that do sound so fair?—I' the name of truth,
Are ye fantastical, or that indeed
Which outwardly ye show?   My noble partner
You greet with present grace, and great prediction
Of noble having, and of ròyal hòpe,
That he seems rapt withal; to me you speak not:
If you can look into the seeds of time,
Speak then to me, who neither beg nor fear
Your favours, nor your hate.
   1 *Witch.* Hail!

2 *Witch.* Hail!

3 *Witch.* Hail!

1 *Witch.* Lesser than Macbeth, and greater.

2 *Witch.* Not so happy, yet much happier.

3 *Witch.* Thou shalt gèt kings, though thou be
    none :

All hail, Macbeth, and Banquo !

   1 *Witch.* Banquo, and Macbeth, all hail!

   Macb. Stay, you imperfect speakers, tell me more:
By Sinel's death, I know I am thane of Glamis ;
But how of Cawdor? the thane of Cawdor lives,
A prosp'rous gentleman; and to be king
Stands not within the prospect of belièf,
No more than to be Cawdor. Say, from whence
You owe this strange intelligence ! or why
Upon this blasted heath you stop our way
With such prophetick greeting?—Speak, I charge
        you.   [*Witches vanish.*

   Ban. The earth hath bubblès, as the water has,
And these are of them.—Whither are they vanish'd ?

   Macb. Into the aìı ; and what seem'd corporal,
    melted
As breath into the wind :—'Would they had stay'd !

   Ban. Were such things hère, as we do speak about!
Or have we eaten of the insane root,
That takes the reason prisoner ?

   Macb. Your children shall be kings.

   Ban.   You shall be king.

   Macb. And thane of Cawdor too ; went it not so ?

 ·*Ban.* To th' selfsame tune, and words. But who
    is here ?

Enter ROSSE *and Others.*

   Rosse. The king hath happily receiv'd, Macbeth,

The news of thy success: and when he reads,
His wonders and his praises do contend,
Which should be thine, or his. As thick as hail,
Came post with post; and every one did bear
Thy praises in his kingdom's great defence,
And pour'd them down before him.

 Ang.   We are sent,
To give thee, from our royal master, thanks.

 Rosse. And, for an earnest of a greater honour,
He bade me, from him, call thee Thane of Cawdor:
In which addition, hail, most worthy thane!

 Macb. The thane of Cawdor lives? Why do you
   dress me
In borrow'd robes?

 Ang.   Who was the thane, lives yet;
But under heavy judgment bears that life
Which he deserves to lose. For treasons prov'd
Have overthrown him.

 Macb.   Glamis, and thane of Cawdor!
The greatest is behind.—Thanks for your pains.—
          . [*To Angus.*
Do you not hope your children shall be kings,
          [*To Banquo.*
When those that gave the thane of Cawdor to me,
Promis'd no less to them?

 Ban.   That, trusted home,
Might yet enkindle you unto the crown:
But oftentimes, to win us to our harm,
The instruments of darkness tell us truths;
Win us with honest trifles, to betray us.
Cousins, a word, I pray.

 Macb.   Two truths are told,
As happy prologues to the swelling act
Of the imperial theme.—I thank you, gentlemen.—

This supernatural soliciting
Cannot be ill; cannot be good :—If ill,
Why hath it given me earnest of success,
Commencing in a truth? I àm thane of Cawdor :
If good, why do I yield to that suggestion
Whose horrid image doth unfix my hair,
And make my seated heart knock at my ribs,
Against the use of nature? Present fears
Are less than horrible imàginings :
My thought, whose murder's yet but fàntasy,
Shakes so my single state of man, that function
Is smother'd in surmise; and nothing is
But what is not.

  Ban.   Look, how our partner's rapt.
  Macb. If chance will have me king, why, chance
   may cròwn me,
Without my stir.
  Ban.   New honours come upon him
Like our strange garments; cleave not to their mould,
But with the aid of use.
  Macb.   Come what come may;
Time and the hour runs through the roughest day.
  Ban. Worthy Macbeth, we stay upon your leisure.
  Macb. Give me your favour :—my dull brain was
   wrought
With things forgot. Kind gentlemen, your pains
Are register'd where ev'ry day I turn
The leaf to read them.—Let us tow'rd the king.—
Think upon what hath chanc'd : and, at more time,
(The interim having weigh'd it), let us speak
Our free hearts each to other.
  Ban.   Very gladly.
  Macb. Till then, enough.—Come, friends.
       [*Exeunt.*

A Room in the Palace.

Flourish. *Enter* DUNCAN, MALCOLM, DONALBAIN, LENOX, *and Attendants.*

Duncan.

S execution done on Cawdor yet?
Are not those in commission yet return'd?
 Mal. They are not yet come back. But
I have spoke
With one that saw him die: who did report,
That very frankly he confess'd his treasons;
Implor'd your highness' pardon; and set forth
A deep repentance. Nothing in his life
Became him, like the leaving it; he died
As one that had been studied in his death,
To throw away the dearest thing he ow'd,
As 'twere a careless trifle.
 Dun.   There's no art,
To find the mind's construction in the fàce:
He was a gentleman on whom I built
An abs'lute trust.

Enter MACBETH, BANQUO, ROSSE, *and* ANGUS.

       O my most worthy cousin!
The sin of my ingratitude ev'n now
Was heavy on me. Would, thou'dst less desèrv'd
That the proportion both of thanks and payment
Might have been mine! I have but left to say,
More is thy dùe than more than all can pay.
 Macb. The service and the loyalty I owe,
In doing, pays itself. Your highness' part
Is to receive our duties: and our duties
Are to your throne and state, children, and servants;

Which do but what they should, by doing every thing
Safe tow'rd your love and honour.

  Dun.   Welcome hither:
I have begun to plant thee, and will labour
To make thee full of growing.—Noble Banquo,
That hast no less deserv'd, nor must be known
No less to hàve done so ; let me enfold thee,
And hold thee to my heart.

  Ban.   There if I grow,
The harvest is your own.

  Dun.   My plenteous joys,
Wanton in fulness, seek to hide themselves
In drops of sorrow.—Sons, kinsmen, and thanes,
And you whose places are the nearest, know,
We will establish our estate upon
Our eldest, Malcolm ; whom we name hereafter,
The prince of Cumberland : which honour must
Not, unaccompanied, invest him only,
But signs of nobleness, like stars, shall shine
On àll deservers.—Hence to Inverness,
And bind us further to you.

  Macb. The rèst is làbour, if not us'd for you :
I'll be myself the hàrbinger, and make
Joyful the hearing of my wìfe
With your approach ; so, humbly take my leave.
       [*Exeunt Duncan and the rest.*
The prince of Cumberland !—That is a step,
On which I must fall down, or else o'erleap ;
For in my way it lies.   Stars, hide your fires !
Let not light see my black and deep desires :
The eye wink at the hand ! yet let that be,
Which the eye fears, when it is done, to see. [*Exit.*

Inverness. *A Room in* Macbeth's *Castle.*

Enter Lady MACBETH, *reading a Letter.*

Lady Macbeth.

THEY met me in the day of success; and I have learn'd by the perfectest report, they have more in them than mortal knowledge. When I burned in desire to question them further, they made themselves—air, into which they vanish'd. Whiles I stood rapt in the wonder of it, came missives from the king, who all-hail'd me, Thane of Cawdor; by which title, before, these weird sisters saluted me, and referr'd me to the coming on of time, with " Hail, king that shalt be !" This have I thought good to deliver thee, my dearest partner of greatness; that thou might'st not lose the dues of rejoicing, by being ignorant of what greatness is promised thee. Lay it to thy heart, and farewell.

Glamis thou art, and Cawdor; and shàlt be
What thou art promis'd :—Yet do I fear thy nature ;
It is too full o' the milk of human kindness,
To catch the nearest way : Thou would'st be grèat ;
Art not without ambition ; but without
The illness should attend it.   Hie thee hither,
That I may pour my spirits in thine ear ;
And chastise with the valour of my tongue
All that impedes thee from the golden round,
Which fate and metaphysical aid doth seem
To have thee crown'd withal.

Enter an Attendant.

What is your tidings ?
Attend. The king comes here to-night.
Lady M.   Thou'rt màd to say it :

Is not thy master with him? who, wer't so,
Would have inform'd for preparàtion.

   Attend. So please you, it is true; our thane is
       coming:
One of my fellows had the speed of him;
Who, almost dead for breath, had scarcely more
Than would make up his message.

   Lady M.   Give him tending,
He brings great news. [*Exit Attendant.*] The raven
       himself is hoarse,
That croaks the fatal entrance of Dùncan
Under my battlements. Come, all you spirits
That tend on mortal thoughts, unsèx me here;
And fill me, from the crown to the toe, top-full
Of direst cruelty! make thick my bloòd,
Stop up th' access and passage to remorse;
That no compunctious visitings of nature
Shake my fell purpose, nor keep peace between
The effect and it! Come to my woman's breasts,
And take my milk for gall, you murd'ring ministers,
Wherever in your sightless substances
You wait on nature's mischief! Come, thick night!
That my keen knife seè not the wound it makes;
Nor heaven peep through the blanket of the dark,
To cry, *Hold, hold!*

             Enter MACBETH.

             Great Glamis! worthy Cawdor!
Greater than both, by the all-hail hereafter!
Thy letters have transported me beyond
This ignorant present time, and I feel now
The future in the instant.

   Macb.   Dearest love,
Duncan comes here to-night.

Lady M.   And when goes hènce?

Macb. To-morrow,—as he purposes.

Lady M.   O, never
Shall sun that morrow sèe!—
Your face, my thane, is as a book, where men
May read strange matters:—To beguile the time,
Look like the time; bear welcome in your eye,
Your hand, your tongue: look like the innocent
    flower,
But bè the serpent under it. He that's coming
Must be provided for: and you shall put
This night's great business into my despatch;
Which shall to all our nights and days to come
Give solely sovereign sway and masterdom.

  Macb. We will speak further.

  Lady M.   Only look up clear;
To alter favour ever is to fear:
Leave all the rest to me.   [*Exeunt.*

Before the Castle.

Hautboys. Servants of Macbeth *attending.*

Enter DUNCAN, MALCOLM, DONALBAIN, BANQUO,
LENOX, MACDUFF, ROSSE, ANGUS, *and Attendants.*

Duncan.

HIS castle hath a pleasant seat: the air
Nimbly and sweetly recommends itself
Unto our senses.

Enter Lady MACBETH.

          See! our honour'd hostess
The love that greets ùs, sometimes is our trouble,

Which still we thank as love.　Herein I teach you,
How you shall bid God-ild us for your pains,
And thank us for your trouble.

　　Lady M.　　　　　　　All our service,
In every point twice done, and then done double,
Were poor and single business, to contend
Against those honours deep and broad, wherewith
Your majesty loads our house: For those of old,
We rest your hermits.

　　Dun.　　　　　　　Where's the thane of Cawdor?
We cours'd him at the heels: but he rides well:
And his great love, sharp as his spur, hath holp him
To 's home before us. Fair and noble hostess,
We are your guest to-night.

　　Lady M.　　　　　　　Your servants ever
Have theirs, themselves, and what is theirs, in compt,
Still to return your own.

　　Dun.　　　　　　　Give me your hand:
Conduct me to mine host:—By your leave, hostess.
　　　　　　　　　　　　　　　　　　[*Exeunt.*

A Room in the Castle.

Enter MACBETH.

Macbeth.

F it were dòne, when 'tis done, then 'twere
　　　well
　　It were done quickly: If the assassination
Could trammel up the consequence, and catch,
With his surcease, success; that but this blow
Might be the be-all and the end-all here:
But hère, upon this bank and shoal of Time,
We'd jump the life to come.　But, in these cases,

We still have judgment here; that we but teach
Bloody instructions, which bèing taught, return
To plague th' inventor: Even handed justice
Commends the ingredients of our poison'd chalice
To our own lips.—He's here in double trust:
First, as I am his kinsman and his subject,
Strong both against the deed; then, as his hòst,
Who should against his murderer shut the door,
Not bear the knife myself.   Besides, this Duncan
Hath borne his faculties so meek, hath been
So clear in his great office, that his virtues
Will plead like angels, trumpet-tongued, against
The deep damnation of his taking off;
And blow the horrid deed in every eye,
That tears shall drown the wind.—I have no spur
To prick the sides of my intent, but only
Vaulting ambition, which o'erleaps ìtself,
And falls on the other side—How now! what news?

Enter Lady MACBETH.

Lady M. He has almost supp'd: Why have you
   left the chamber?
Macb. Hath he ask'd for me?
Lady M.   Knòw you not, he has?
Macb. We will proceed no further in this business.
He hath honour'd me of late: and I have bought .
Golden opinions from all sorts of people,
Which would be worn now in their newest gloss,
Not cast aside so soon.
Lady M.   Was the hope drunk,
Wherein you dress'd yourself? hath it slèpt since?
And wakes it now, to look so green and pale
At what it did so freely?   From this time,
Such I account thy lòve.   Art thou afeard

B

To be the same in thine own act and valour,
As thou art in desire ?   Would'st thou have that
Which thou esteem'st the ornament of life,
And live a coward in thine own esteem ;
Letting I dare not wait upon I would,
Like the poor cat i' the adage ?

Macb.   Pr'ythee, peace :
I dare do all that may becòme a man ;
Who dares do more, is none.

Lady M.   What beast was't then,
That made you break this enterprise to me ?
When you durst do it, then you wère a man ;
And, to be mòre than what you were, you would
Be so much more the man.   Nor time, nor place,
Did then cohere, and yet you would make both ;
They have made themselves, and that their fitness,
        now
Does unmake yòu.

Macb.   If we should fàil !
Lady M.   We fail.
But screw your courage to the sticking-place,
And we'll nòt fail.   When Duncan is asleep
(Whereto the rather shall his day's hard journey
Soundly invite him), his two chamberlains
Will I with wine and wassel so convince,
That memory, the warder of the brain,
Shall be a fume ; and when in swinish sleep
Their drenched natures lie, as in a death,
What cannot you and I perform upon
The unguarded Duncan? what not put upon
His spongy officers ; who shall bear the guilt
Of our great quell ?

Macb.   Bring forth men-children only !
For thy undaunted mettle shòuld compose

Nothing but males. Will it not be receiv'd,
When we have mark'd with blood those sleepy two
Of his own chámber, and us'd their very daggers,
That they hàve done't?

   Lady M. Who dares receive it other,
As we shall make our griefs and clamour roar
Upon his death?

   Macb. I'm settled, and bend up
Each corporal agent to this terrible feat.
Away, and mock the time with fairest show:
False face must hide what the false heart doth know.

                         [Exeunt.

ACT II.

Court within the Castle.

Enter BANQUO *and* FLEANCE, *and a Servant, with a Torch before them.*

Banquo.

OW goes the night, boy?

   Fle. The moon is down: I have not heard
      the clock.

   Ban. And she goes down at twelve.

   Fle. 'Tis làter, sir.

   Ban. Hold, take my sword:—There's husbandry
      in heaven,
Their candles are all out.—Take thee that too.
A heavy summons lies like lead upon me,
And yet I would not sleep: Merciful powers!
Restrain in me the cursed thoughts, that nature
Gives way to in repose:—Who's there?

Enter MACBETH, *and a Servant with a Torch.*

Macb.   A friend.

Ban. What, sir, not yet at rest? The king's a-bed:
He hath been in unusual pleasure, and
Sent forth great largess to your officers.
This diamond he greets your wife withal,
By the name of most kind hostess; and's shut up
In measureless content.—All's very well.
I dream'd last night of the three weird sisters:
To you they've show'd some truth.

Macb.   I think not of them:
Yet, when we can entreat an hour to serve,
Would spend it in some wòrds upon that business,
If you would grant the time.

Ban.   At your kind leisure
I shall be counsel'd.

Macb.   Good repose, the while.

Ban. Thanks, sir; The like to you!
                    [*Exeunt Banquo and Fleance.*

Macb. Go, bid thy mistress, when my drink is ready,
She strike upon the bell.   Get thee to bed.
                            [*Exit Servant.*

Is this a dagger, which I see before me,
The handle toward my hand? Còme, let me clutch
        thee:
I have thee not, and yet I see thee still.
Art thou not, fatal vision, sensible
To feeling, as to sìght? or art thou but
A dagger of the mìnd; a false creation,
Proceeding from the heat-oppressed brain?
I see thee yèt, in form as palpable
As this which now I draw.
Thou marshal'st me the way that I was going;

And such an instrument I was to use.
Mine eyes are made the fools o' the other senses,
Or else worth all the rest : I see thee still ;
And on thy blade and dudgeon, gouts of blood,
Which was not so before.—There's no such thing :
It is the bloody business, which informs
Thus to mine eyes.—Now o'er the one half world
Nature seems dead, and wicked dreams abuse
The curtain'd sleep ; now witchcraft celebrates
Pale Hecate's offerings ; and wither'd murder,
Alarum'd by his sentinel, the wolf,
·Whose howl's his watch, thus with his stealthy pace,
Moves like a ghost.——Thou sure and firm-set earth,
Hear not my steps, which way they walk, for fear
Thy very stones prate of my where-about,
And take the present horror from the time,
Which now suits with it.—Whiles I threat, he lives.
                    [*A bell rings.*
I go, and it is done ; the bell invites me.
Hear it not, Duncan ; for it is a knell
That summons thee to heaven, or to hell.   [*Exit.*

Enter Lady MACBETH.

Lady M. That which hath made them drunk, hath
    made me bold :
What hath quench'd them, hath given me fire :—hark !
It was the owl that shriek'd, the fatal bellman,
Which gives the stern'st good night.—He is about it :
The doors are open ; and the surfeited grooms
Do mock their charge with snores : I've drugg'd their
        possets,
That death and nature do contend about them,
Whether they live or die.
    Macb. [*Within.*]   Who's there ?—what, hoa !

Lady M. Alack ! I am afraid they have awak'd,
And 'tis not done :—the attempt and not the deèd
Confoùnds us :—Hark !—I laid their daggers ready,
He could not miss 'em.   Had he not resembled
My father as he slept, I had done't.—My husband !

Enter MACBETH.

   Macb. I've done the deed :—Didst thou not hear
     a noise ?
   Lady M. I heard the owl scream, and the crickets
     cry.
Did not you speak ?
   Macb.   When ?
   Lady M.   Now.
   Macb.   As I descended ?
   Lady M. Ay.
   Macb. This is a sorry sight. [*Looking on his hands.*
   Lady M. A foolish thought, to say a sorry sight.
   Macb. There's one did laugh in 's sleep,
And one cried, *Murder !* that they wak'd each other;
I stood and heard them : but they did say their prayers,
And address'd them again to sleep.
One cried, *God bless us !* and, *Amen,* the other ;
As they had seen me, with these hangman's hands.
Listening their fear.—I could not say, " Amen,"
When they did say, God bless us.
   Lady M. Consider it not so deeply.
   Macb. But wherefore could not I pronounce, Amen?
I had most need of blessing, and Amen
Stuck in my throat.
   Lady M.   These deeds must not be thought on
After these ways ; so, it will make us màd.
    Macb. Methought, I heard a voice cry, "Sleep no
     more !

Macbeth does murder sleep !"

    Lady M.   What do you mean ?

    Macb. Still it cried, "Sleep no more !" to all the
        house :

"Glamis hath murder'd sleep; and therefore Cawdor

Shall sleep no more. Macbeth shall sleep no more!"

    Lady M. Who was it that thus cried? Why, worthy
        thane,

You do unbend your noble strength, to think

So brainsickly of things : Go, get some water,

And wash this filthy witness from your hand.—

Why did you bring these daggers from the place ?

They must lie thère : Go, carry them'; and smear

The sleepy grooms with blood.

    Macb.   I'll go no more :

I am afraid to think what I have done ;

Look on't again, I dare not.

    Lady M.   Infirm of purpose !

Give me the daggers : The sleeping, and the dead,

Are but as pictures : 'tis the eye of childhood,

That fears a painted devil. If he bleed,

I'll gild the faces of the grooms withal,

For it must seem their guilt.

                [*Exit. Knocking within.*

    Macb.   Whence is that knocking ?

How is't with me, when every noise appals me ?

What hands are here ! Ha! they pluck out mine eyes !

Will all great Neptune's ocean wash this blood

Clean from my hand ? No ; this my hand will rather

The multitudinous seas incarnardine,

Making the green—one red.

        Re-enter Lady MACBETH.

    Lady M. My hànds are of your colour; but I shame

To wear a hèart so whìte. [*Knock.*] I hear a knocking
At the south entry :—retire we to our chamber :
A little water clears us of this deed :
Get on your nightgown, lest occasion call us,
And show us to be watchers :—Be not lost
So poorly in your thoughts.

    Macb. To know my deèd, 'twere best not know
      mysèlf.   [*Knock.*
Wàke Duncan with this knocking! Would thou
      could'st ?   [*Exeunt.*

The same.

Enter MACDUFF, LENOX, *and a Porter.*

Macduff.

S thy master stirring?—
Our knocking has awak'd him; here he
comes.

Enter MACBETH.

Len. Good-morrow, noble sir!
Macb.   Good-morrow, both!
Macd. Is the king stirring, worthy thane?
Macb.   Not yet.
Macd. He did command me to call timely on him;
I have almost slipp'd the hour.
    Macb.   I'll bring you to him.
    Macd. I know, this is a joyful trouble to you;
But yet, 'tis one.
    Macb. The labour we delight in physicks pain.
This is the door.
    Macd.   I'll make so bold to call,
For 'tis my limited service.   [*Exit Macduff.*
    Len. Goes the king hence to-day?

Macb. He does : he did appoint so.

Len. The night has been unruly : Where we lay,
Our chimneys were blown down ; and, as they say,
Lamentings heard i' the air; strange screams of death :
Some say, the earth was feverous, and did shake.

Macb. 'Twas a rough night.

Len. My young remembrance cannot parallel
A fellow to it.

Re-enter MACDUFF.

Macd. O horror! horror! horror! Tongue, nor
     heart,
Cannot conceive, nor name thee!

Macb. Len.   What's the matter?

Macd. Confusion now hath made his masterpiece!
Most sacrilegious murder hath broke ope
The Lord's anointed temple, and stole thence
The life o' the building.

Macb.   What is't you say? the life?

Len. Mean you his majesty?

Macd. Approach the chamber :—Do not bid me
     speak ;
See, and then speak yourselves.—Awake! awake!—
               [*Exeunt Macbeth and Lenox.*
Ring the alarum-bell :—Murder! and treason!
Banquo, and Donalbain! Malcolm! awake!
Shake off this downy sleep, death's counterfeit,
And look on death itself!——Malcolm and Donal-
     bain!
As from your graves rise up, and walk like sprites,
To countenance this horror!—Ring the bell.
                    [*Bell rings.*

Enter BANQUO.

O Banquo! Banquo! our royal master's murder'd!

Re-enter MACBETH *and* LENOX.

Macb. Had I but died an hour before this chance,
I had liv'd a blessed time ; for, from this instant,
There's nothing serious in mortality.

Enter MALCOLM *and* DONALBAIN.

Don. What is amiss?
Macb.   You are, and do not know't:
The spring, the head, the fountain of your blood
Is stòpp'd ; the very source of it is stopp'd.
Macd. Your royal father's murder'd.
Mal.   O, by whom?
Len. Those of his chamber, as it seem'd, had done't:
Their hands and faces were all badg'd with blood,
So were their daggers, which, unwip'd, we found
Upon their pillows: they star'd, and were distract.
Macb. O, yet I do repent me of my fury,
That I did kill them.
Macd.   Whèrefore did you so?
Macb. Who can be wise, amaz'd, temperate, and
          furious,
Loyal and neutral, in a moment? No man :
The expedition of my violent love
Outran the pauser reason.—Here lay Duncan,
His silver skin lac'd with his golden blood ;
And his gash'd stabs look'd like a breach in nature,
For ruin's wasteful entrance : there, the murderers,
Steep'd in the colours of their trade, their daggers
Unmannerly breech'd with gore : Who could re-
          frain,
That had a heart to love, and in that heart
Courage, to make 's love known?
Lady.   Help me hence, ho !

Macd. Look to the lady.　　　[*She is carried out.*

Ban.　　　　　　Fears and scruples shake us :

In the great hand of God I stand : and, thence,

Against the undivulg'd pretence I fight

Of treasonous malice.

Macd.　　　　　So do I.

All.　　　　　　　　　So all.

Macb. Let's briefly put on manly readiness,

And meet i' the hall together.

All.　　　　　　　　Well contented.

　　　　　[*Exeunt all but Mal. and Don.*

ACT III.

A Room in the Palace.

Enter BANQUO.

Banquo.

THOU hast it now, King, Cawdor, Glamis, all,

As the weird women promis'd ; and, I fear,

Thou play'dst most foully for it.　Hush !

no more.

Senet sounded.　Enter MACBETH, *as*　King ; Lady
MACBETH, *as* Queen ; LENOX, ROSSE, *Lords, Ladies, and Attendants.*

Macb. Here's our chief guest.

Lady M.　　　　　If he had been forgotten,

It had been as a gap in our great feast,

And all-things unbecoming.

Macb. To-night we hold a solemn supper, sir,

And I'll request your presence.

Ban.　　　　　　Lay your highness'

Commànd upon me ; to the which, my duties
Are with a most indissoluble tie
For ever knit.
 Macb.   Ride you this afternoon?
 Ban. Ay, my good lord.
 Macb.   We should have else desir'd
Your good advice in this day's council ; but
We'll tak't to-morrow. Is it far you ride?
 Ban. As far, my lord, as will fill up the time
'Twixt this and supper. Go not my horse the better,
I must become a borrower of the night,
For a dark hour, or twain.
 Macb.   Fail not our feast.
 Ban. My lord, I will not.
 Macb. Hie to horse : Adieu,
Till you return at night !—Goes Fleance with you?
 Ban. Ay my good lord : our time does call upon us.
 Macb. I wish your horses swift, and sure of foot ;
And so I do commend you to their backs.
Farewell.   [*Exit Banquo.*
Let every man be master of his time
Till seven at night ; to make society
The sweeter welcome, we will keep ourself,
Till supper-time, alone : till then farewell.
  [*Exeunt Lady Macbeth, Lords, Ladies, &c.*
Sirrah, a word with you : attend those men
Our pleasure?
 Atten. They are, my lord, without the palace gate.
 Macb. Bring them before us.— [*Exit Atten.*
    To be thus is nòthing ;
But to be sàfely thus :—Our fears in Banquo
Stick deep ; and in his royalty of nature
Reigns that which would be fear'd. He chid the
  sisters,
When first they put the name of King upon me,

And bade them speak to him; then, prophet-like,
They hail'd him father to a line of kings.
Upon my head they plac'd a fruitless crown,
Thence to be wrench'd with an unlineal hand,
No son of mine succèeding.   If't be so,
For Banquo's issùe have I fil'd my mind;
For thèm the gracious Duncan have I murder'd;
To make them kings; the seed of Banquo kings!
Rather than so, come fate into the list,
And champion me to the utterance !—Who's there?—

Re-enter Attendant *with two* Murderers.

Was it not yesterday we spoke together?
   1 *Mur.* It was, so please your highness.
   Macb.   Well then, now,
Have you consider'd?
   2 *Mur.*   'I am one, my liege,
Whom the vile blows and buffets of the world
Have so incens'd, that I am reckless what
I do, to spite the world.
   1 *Mur.*   And I another,
So weary with disasters, tugg'd with fortune,
That I would set my life on any chance,
To mend it, or be rid on't.
   Macb.   Both of you
Know, Banquo was yòur enemy.
   2 *Mur.*   True, my lord.
   Macb. So is he mine: and in such bloody distance,
That every mìnute of his bèing thrusts
Against my near'st of life : And though I could
With bare-fac'd power sweep him from my sight,
And bid my will avòuch it; yet I must not,
For sundry weighty reasons.
   2 *Mur.*   We shall, my lord,
Perform what you command us.

1 *Mur.*   Though our lives——
Macb. Your spirits shine through you. Within this
        hour
I will advise you where to plant yourselves :
Acquaint you with the perfect spy o' th' time,
The moment on't.   Resolve yourselves apart ;
I'll come to you anon.
    2 *Mur.*   We àre resolv'd.
    Macb. I'll call upon you straight ; abide within.
It is concluded :——Banquo, thy soul's flight,
If it find heaven, must find it out to-night.
                                 [*Exeunt Murderers.*

Enter Lady MACBETH.

Lady M. How now, my lord? why do you keep
        alone,
Using those thoughts, which should indeed have died
With them they think on ?   Things without remedy
Should be without regard : what's done, is done.
    Macb. We have scotch'd the snake, not kill'd it ;
She'll close, and be herself ; whilst our poor malice
Remains in danger of her former tooth.
But let both worlds disjoint, and all things suffer,
Ere we will eat our meal in fear, and sleep
In the affliction of these terrible dreams
That shake us nightly.   Better be with the dèad,
Whom we, to gain our place, have sent to peace,
Than on the torture of the mind to lie
In restless ecstasy.   Duncan is in his grave ;
After life's fitful fever, he sleeps well :
Treason has done his worst ; nor steel, nor poison,
Malice domestic, foreign levy, nothing
Can touch him further !
    Lady M.   Come on ; gentle lord,

Sleek o'er your rugged looks; you must leave this.

Macb. O, full of scorpions is my mind, dear wife !
Thou know'st, that Banquo, and his Fleance, live.

Lady M. But in them nature's copy not eterne.

Macb. There's comfort yet, they are assailable;
Then be thou jocund: Ere the bat hath flown
His cloister'd flight; ere, to black Hecate's summons,
The shard-borne beetle, with his drowsy hum,
Hath rung night's yawning peal, there shall be done
A deed of dreadful note.

Lady M. What's to be done?

Macb. Be innocent of the knowledge, dearest chuck,
Till thou applaud the deed. Come, seeling night!
Good things of day begin to droop and drowse;
While night's black agents to their preys do rouse.
Thou marvell'st at my words; but hold thee still;
Things, bad begun, make strong themselves by ill.

[*Exeunt.*

A Room of State in the Palace.

A Banquet prepared.

Enter MACBETH, Lady MACBETH, ROSSE, LENOX,
Lords, and Attendants.

Macbeth.

YOU know your own degrees, sit down: at
first
And last, a hearty welcome.

Lords. Thanks to your majesty.

Macb. Ourself will mingle with society:
Our hostess keeps her state; but, in best time,

We will require her welcome.

Lady M. Pronounce it for me, sir, to all our friends;
For my heàrt speaks, they're welcome.

Enter first Murderer, *to the door.*

Macb. See, they encounter thee with thèir hearts'
          thanks :——
Both sides are even : Here I'll sit i' the midst.
Be large in mirth; anon, we'll drink a measure
The table round.—There's blood upon thy face.

Mur. 'Tis Banquo's then.   [*Aside, at the door.*
Macb. Is he despatch'd?
Mur.   My Lord, his throat is cut.
Macb. Thou art the best o' the cut-throats : Yet
          he's good
That did the like for Fleance.

Mur.   Royal sir,
Fleance is 'scap'd.

Macb. Then comes my 'fit again: I had else been
          perfect;
Whole as the marble, founded as the rock;
But now, I am cabin'd, cribb'd, confin'd, bound in
To saucy doubts and fears.   But Banquo's safe?

Mur. Ay, my good lord: safe in a ditch he bides,
With twenty trenched gashes on his head;
The least a death to nature.

Macb.   Thanks for that :——
There the gròwn serpent lies.   [*Exit Murderer.*

Lady M.   My royal lord,
You do not give the cheer: the feast is cold,
That is not often vouched while 'tis making;
'Tis given with welcome: To feed were best at home;
Fròm thence, the saùce to meat is ceremony;
Meeting were bare without it.

Macb.   Sweet remembrancer!—
Now, good digestion wait on appetite,
And health on both!
   Len.   May 't please your highness sit?

The Ghost *of* BANQUO *sits in* MACBETH'S *place.*

Macb. The table's full.   [*Starting.*
Len.   Here is a place reserv'd, sir.
Macb. Where?
Len.   Here, my lord.   What is't that moves
      your highness?
Macb. Which of you have done this?
Lords.   .   Whàt, my good lord?
Macb. Thou canst not say, I did it: never shake
Thy gory locks at me.
   Rosse. Gentlemen, rise; his highness is not well.
   Lady M. Sìt, worthy friends:—my lord is often
      thus;
The fit is momentary: If you note him,
You shall offend him, and extend his passion;
Feed, and regard him not.—Are you a man? [*Aside.*
   Macb. Ay, and a bold one, that dare look on that
Which might appal the devil.
   Lady M.   Proper stuff!
This is the very painting of your fear:
This is the air-drawn dagger, which, you said,
Led you to Duncan.   O, these flaws, and starts,
(Impostors to true fear), would well become
A woman's story at a winter's fire,
Authoriz'd by her grandam.   When all's done,
You look but on a stool.
   Macb. Pr'ythee, see there! behold! look! lo!
      how say you?——
Why, what care I? If thou canst nod, spèak too.—

If charnel-houses and our graves, must send
Those that we bury back, our monuments
Shall be the maws of kites.   [*Ghost disappears.*
   Lady M.   What! quite unmann'd?
   Macb. If I stand here, I saw him.
   Lady M.   Fye, for shame!
   Macb. Blood hath been shed ere now, i' the olden
      time;
Ay, and since too, murders have been perform'd
Too terrible for the ear: the times have been,
That when the brains were out the man would die
And there an end: but now, they rise again,
With twenty mortal murders on their crowns,
And push us from our stools.
   Lady M.   My worthy lord,
Your noble friends do lack you.
   Macb.   I forget :—
Do not muse at me, my most worthy friends;
I have a strange infirmity, which is nothing
To those that know me.   Love and health to all;
Then I'll sit down:—Give me some wine, fill full:—
I drink to the general joy of the whole table,

Enter Ghost.

And to our dear friend Banquo, whom we miss;
'Would he were here! to all, and him, we thirst.—
Avaunt! and quit my sight! Let the earth hide thee!
Thy bones are marrowless, thy blood is cold;
Thou hast no speculation in those eyes
Which thou dost glare with!
   Lady M.   Think of this, good peers,
But as a thing of custom: 'tis no other..
   Macb. What man dare, I dare:
Approach thou like the rugged Russian bear,

The arm'd rhinoceros, or the Hyrcan tiger,
Take any shape but thàt, and my firm nerves
Shall never tremble : Or, be alive again,
And dare me to the desert with thy sword :
If trembling, I inhibit, then protest me
The baby of a girl.—Hence, horrible shadow !
Unreal mockery, hence !—[*Ghost disappears.*] Why,
    so ;—being gone,
I am a man again.—'Pray you, sit still. [*They rise.*
  Lady M. You have displac'd the mirth, broke the
    good meeting,
With most admir'd disorder.
  Macb.   Can such things be,
And overcome us like a summer's cloud,
Without our special wonder? You make me strange
Even to the disposition that I owe,
When now I think yòu can behold such sights,
And keep the natural ruby of your cheeks,
When mine are blanch'd with fear.
  Rosse.   What sights, my lord ?
  Lady M. I pray you, speak not ; he grows worse
    and worse ;
Question enràges him : at once, good night :—
Stand not upon the order of your going,
But go at once.
  Len.   Good night, and better health
Attend his majesty !
  Lady M.   A kind good night to all !
          [*Exeunt Lords and Attendants.*
  Macb. It will have blood ; they say, blood will
    have blood !
Stones have been known to move, and trees to speak ;
Augurs, and understood relations, have brought forth
The secret'st man of blood.—What is the night ?

Lady M. Almost at odds with morning, which is
 which.

Macb. How say'st thou, that Macduff denies his
 person,
At our great bidding?

Lady M.   Did you send to him?

Macb. I hear it by the way; but I will send:
There's not a Thane of them, but in his house
I keep a servant fee'd. I will to-morrow
To the weird sisters; for I'm bent to know,
By the worst mèans, the worst: I am in blood
Stept in so far, that, should I wade no more,
Returning were as tedious as go o'er.

Lady M. You lack the season of all natures, sleep.

Macb. Come, we'll to sleep: My strange and
 self-abuse
Is the initiate fear, that wants hard use:—
We are yet but young in deed.   [*Exeunt.*

ACT IV.

*A dark Cave. In the middle, a Cauldron
boiling.*

Thunder. Enter the three Witches.

1 *Witch.*

THRICE the brinded cat hath mew'd.
 2 *Witch.* Thrice; and once the hedge-pig
  whin'd.

 1 *Witch.* Round about the cauldron go;

In the poison'd entrails throw.
Toad, that under the cold stone,
Days and nights has thirty-one,
Swelt'ring venom, sleeping got,
Boil thou first i' the charmed pot!

All. Double, double toil and trouble;
Fire burn; and cauldron bubble.

2 *Witch.* Fillet of a fenny snake,
In the cauldron boil and bake:
Eye of newt, and toe of frog,
Wool of bat, and tongue of dog,
Adder's fork, and blind-worm's sting,
Lizard's leg, and owlet's wing,
For a charm of pow'rful trouble,
Like a hell-broth boil and bubble.

All. Double, double toil and trouble;
Fire burn; and cauldron bubble.

3 *Witch.* Scale of dragon, tooth of wolf,
Witches mummy; maw and gulf
Of the rav'ning salt-sea shark;
Root of hemlock digg'd i' the dark;
Liver of blaspheming Jew;
Gall of goat; and slips of yew
Sliver'd in the moon's eclipse;
Nose of Turk, and Tartar's lips;
Add thereto a tiger's chauldron,
For the ingredients of our cauldron.

All. Double, double, toil and trouble;
Fire burn; and cauldron bubble.

2 *Witch.* Cool it with a baboon's blood,
Then the charm is firm and good.

Musick and a Song. *Black Spirits, &c.*

2 *Witch.* By the pricking of my thumbs,

Something wicked this way comes :—.
Open, locks, whoever knocks.

Enter MACBETH.

Macb. How now, you secret, black, and midnight
    hags?
What is't you do?
   All.   A deed without a name.
   Macb. I cónjure you, by that which you profess,
(Howe'er you come to know it), answer me
To what I ask you.
   1 *Witch.*   Speak.
   2 *Witch.*   Demand.
   3 *Witch.*   We'll answer.
   1 *Witch.* Say, if thou'dst rather hear it from our
    mouths,
Or from our masters'?
   Macb.   Call 'em, let me see 'em.
   1 *Witch.* Pour in sow's blood !
   All. Come high, come low ;
    Thyself and office deftly show.

   Thunder.   1 Apparition, *of an armed Head.*

   Macb. Tell me, thou unknown power,—
   1 *Witch.*   He knows thy thought ;
Hear his spèech, but sày thou nought.
   App. Macbeth ! Macbeth ! Macbeth ! beware
    Macduff ;
Beware the thane of Fife.—Dismiss me :—Enough.
   Macb. Thou hast harp'd my fear aright :—But one
    word more :—
   1 *Witch.* He will not be commanded : Here's an-
    other,
More potent than the first.

Thunder. 2 Apparition, *of a bloody Child.*

App. Macbeth! Macbeth! Macbeth!
Be bloody, bold, and resolute; laugh to scorn
The power of man, for none of woman born
Shall harm Macbeth. [*Descends.*

Macb. Then live, Macduff; What need I fear of
    thee?
But yet I'll make assurance double sure,
And take a bond of fate: thou shalt not live;
That I may tell pale-hearted fear it lies,
And sleep in spite of thunder.—What is this,
That rises like the issue of a king;
And wears upon his baby brow the round
.And top of sovereignty? [3 *Apparition.*

All. Listen; speak not.

App. Be lion-mettled, proud; and take no care
Who chafes, who frets, or where conspirers are;
Macbeth shall never vanquish'd be, until
Great Birnam wood to high Dunsinane hill
Shall come against him.

Macb. That will never be;
Who can impress the forest; bid the tree
Unfix his earth-bound root? Sweet bodements! good!
Yet tell me this, shall Banquo's issue ever
Reign in this kingdom?

All. Seek to know no more.

Macb. I will be satisfied: deny me this,
And an eternal curse fall on you! Let me know:—
Why sinks that cauldron? and what noise is this?
[*Hautboys.*

1 *Witch.* Show! 2 *Witch.* Show! 3 *Witch.* Show!
All. Show his eyes, and grieve his heart;
Come like shadows, so depart.

A show of Eight Kings, and BANQUO *last, with a Glass in his Hand.*

Macb. Thou art too like the spirit of Banquo;
　　down!

Thy crown does sear mine eyeballs:—And thy air,
Thou other gold-bound brow, is like the first:—
A third is like the former:—Filthy hags!
Why do you show me this?—A fourth?—Start, eyes!
What! will the line stretch out to th' crack of doom?
Another yet?—A seventh!—I'll see no more:—
And yet the eighth appears, who bears a glass,
Which shows me many more.—I see, 'tis true;
For the blood-bolter'd Banquo smiles upon me,
And points at them for his.—What! is this so?

　　　　　[*Musick. The Witches dance, and vanish.*

Macb. Where are they? Gone?—Let this perni-
　　cious hour

Stand aye accursed in the calendar!—
Come in, without there!

Enter LENOX.

Len.　　　　　　　　What's your grace's will?
Macb. Saw you the weird sisters?
Len.　　　　　　　　　　No, my lord;
Macb. Came they not by you?
Len.　　　　　　　　　　No, indeed, my lord.
Macb. Infected be the air whereon they ride;
And damn'd all those that trust them!—I did hear
The galloping of horse: Who was't came by?
Len. 'Tis two or three, my lord, that bring you
　　word,
Macduff is fled to England.
Macb. Time, thou anticipat'st my dread exploits:
The castle of Macduff I will surprise;

Seize upon Fife; give to the edge o' the sword
His wife, his babes : no boasting like a fool :
This deed I'll do, before this purpose cool. [*Exeunt.*

England. *A Room in the King's Palace.*

Enter MALCOLM *and* MACDUFF.

Malcolm.

ET us seek out some desolate shade, and
there
Weep our sad bosoms empty.

Macd.   Let us rather
Hold fast the mortal swòrd ; and, like good men,
Bestride our downfall'n birthdom. Each new morn,
New widows howl; new orphans cry; new sorrows
Strike heaven on the face, that it resounds
As if it felt with Scotland.

Mal.   And this tyrant
Was once thought honest : you have lov'd him well;
He hath not touch'd you yet.

Macd.   I've lost my hopes.

Mal. Why in that rawness left you wife and child,
Without leave-taking ? Yet you may be just,
Whatever I shall think.

Macd.   Bleed, bleed, poor country !
Great tyranny, lay thou thy basis sure,
For goodness dares not check thee !—Fare thee well,
I would not be the villain that thou think'st
For the whole space that's in the tyrant's grasp,
And the rich East to boot.

Mal.   Be not offended :

I think our country sinks beneath the yoke ;
And here, from gracious England, have I offer
Of goodly thousands : But yet for all this,
When I shall tread upon the tyrant's head,
Or wear it on my sword, yet my poor country
Shall have more vices than it had before ;
By him that shall succeed.

 Macd.   What should he be ?

 Mal. It is myself I mean : in whom I know
All the particulars of vice so grafted,
That, when they shall be open'd, black Macbeth
Will seem as pure as snow, being compar'd
With my confineless harms.

 Macd.   O Scotland ! Scotland !

 Mal. If such a one be fit to govern, speak :
I am as I have spoken.

 Macd.   Fit to govern !
No, not to live.—O nation miserable,
When shalt thou see thy wholesome days again ?
Since that the truest issue of thy throne
By his own interdiction stands accurs'd ?
Thy hope ends here !

 Mal.   Macduff, this noble passion,
Child of integrity, hath from my soul
Wip'd the black scruples, reconcil'd my thoughts
To thy good truth and honour. Even now
I put myself to thy direction, and
Unspeak mine own detraction : here abjure
The taints and blames I laid upon myself,
For strangers to my nature. What I am
Is thine, and my poor country's, to command.

 Macd. Such welcome and unwelcome things at
    once,
'Tis hard to reconcile.

Enter ROSSE.

                      See, who comes here?

Mal. My countryman; but yet I know him not.

Macd. My ever-gentle cousin, welcome hither.
Stands Scotland where it did?

Rosse.   Alas, poor country!
Almost afraid to know itself! where nothing,
But who knòws nothing, is once seen to smile; ·
Where sighs are made, not mark'd; the dead man's
    ·   knell
Is there scarce ask'd, for whom; and good men's lives
Expire before the flowers in their caps,
Dying or ere they sicken.

Macd. ·   O, relation
Too nice, and yet too true! How does my wife?

Rosse. Why, well.

Macd.   ·   And all my children?

Rosse.   All well too.

Macd. The tyrant has not batter'd at their peace?

Rosse. No; they were well at peàce, when I did
    leave them.

Macd. Be not a niggard of your speech; How
    goes it?

Rosse. When I came hither to transport the tidings,
Which I have heavily borne, there ran a rumour
Of many worthy fellows that were out.
Now is the time of help! your eye in Scotland
Would creàte soldiers, make our wòmen fight,
To doff their dire distresses.

Mal.   Be't their comfort,
We are coming thither.

Rosse.   'Would, that I could answer
This comfort with the like! But I have words,
That would be howl'd out in the desert air,

Where hearing should not catch them.

    Macd.   What? concern they
The general cause? or is it a fee-grief,
Due to some single breast?

    Rosse.   No mind, that's honest,
But in it shares some woe; though the main part
Pertains to you alone.

    Macd.   If it be mine,
Keep it not from me, quickly let me have it.

    Rosse. Let not your ears despise my tongue for
        ever,
Which shall possess them with the heaviest sound
That ever yet they heard.

    Macd.   Ha! I guess at it.

    Rosse. Your castle is surprised; your wife, and
        babes
Savagely slaughter'd: to relate the manner,
Were, on the quarry of these murder'd deer,
To add the death of you.

    Mal.   Merciful heaven!—
What, man! ne'er pull your hat upon your brows;
Give sorrow words: the grief, that does not speak,
Whispers the o'erfraught heart, and bids it break.

    Macd. My children too?

    Rosse.   Wife, children, servants, all
That could be found.

    Macd.   And I must be from thence!
My wife kill'd too?

    Rosse.   I've said.

    Mal.   Be comforted:
Let's make us med'cines of our great revenge,
To cure this deadly grief.

    Macd.   He has no children.
What, all my pretty ones? did you say, all?

What, all my pretty chickens, and their dam,
At one fell swoop?

Mal. Dispute it like a man.

Macd.   I shall do so;
But I must also feel it as a man;
I cannot but remember such things were,
That were most precious to me.—Did heaven look on,
And would not take their part? Sinful Macduff,
They were all struck for thee! naught that I am,
Not for their own demerits, but for mine,
Fell slaughter on their souls.—Heaven rest them now!

Mal. Be this the whetstone of your sword: let grief
Convert to wrath; blunt not the heart, enrage it.

Macd. O, I could play the woman with mine eyes,
And braggart with my tongue!—But, gentle heaven,
Cut short all intermission: front to front,
Bring thou this fiend of Scotland, and myself;
Within my sword's length set him; if he 'scape,
Then Heaven forgive him too!

ACT V.

Dunsinane. *A Room in the Castle.*

Enter a Doctor *of Physick, and a waiting*
Gentlewoman.

Doctor.

 HAVE two nights watched with you, but
can perceive no truth in your report. When
was it she last walked?

Gent. Since his majesty went into the field, I have

seen her rise from her bed, throw her night-gown upon her, unlock her closet, take forth paper, fold it, write upon it, read it, afterwards seal it, and again return to bed; yet all this while in a most fast sleep.

Enter Lady MACBETH, *with a Taper.*

Lo you, here she comes! Observe her; stand close.

Doct. How came she by that light?

Gent. She has light by her continually: 'tis her command.

Doct. You see her eyes are open.

Gent. Ay, but their sènse is shut.

Doct. Look, how she rubs her hands.

Lady M. Yet here's a spot. Out, damnĕd spot! out, I say!—One: Two: Why, then 'tis time to do't:——Hell is murky!—Fye, my lord, fye! a soldier, and afeard? What need we fear who knows it, when none can call our power to account?—Yet who would have thought the old man to have had so much blood in him?

Doct. Do you mark that?

Lady M. The thane of Fife had a wife: Where is shè now?——What, will these hands ne'er be clean? —No more o' that, my lord, no more o' that: you mar all with this starting.—Here's the smèll of the blood still: all the perfumes of Arabia will not sweeten this little hand. Oh!—oh!—oh!

Doct. What a sigh is there! The heart is sorely charged.

Gent. I would not have such a heart in my bosom, for the dignity of the whole body.

Lady M. Wash your hands, put on your night-gown; look not so pale:—I tell you yet again, Banquo's bùried; he cannot come out of his grave. To bed, to bed; there's knocking at the gate. Come, come, come, come, give me your hand; What's done, cannot be undone: To bed, to bed, to bed.

[*Exit Lady Macbeth.*

Doct. Will she go now to bed?

Gent. Directly.

Doct. Foul whisp'rings are abroad: Infected minds
To their deaf pillows will discharge their secrets.
More needs she the divine, than the physician.—
Remove from her the means of all annoyance,
And still keep eyes upon her:—So, good night:
I think, but dare not speak.

Gent. Good night, good doctor.

[*Exeunt.*

Dunsinane. *A Room in the Castle.*

Enter MACBETH, Doctor, *and Attendants.*

Macbeth.

RING me no more reports; let them fly all
Till Birnam wood remove to Dunsinane,
I cannot taint with fear. What's the boy
Malcolm?
Was he not born of woman? The spirits that know
All mortal consequences, have pronounc'd me thus:
*Fear not, Macbeth; no man, that's born of woman,
Shall e'er have power upon thee.*——Fly, false thanes,
And mingle with the English epicures!
The mind I sway by, and the heart I bear,
Shall never sagg with doubt, nor shake with fear.

Enter a Servant.

The devil damn thee black, thou cream-fac'd loon!
Where got'st thou that goose look?

Serv. There is ten thousand——

Macb. Gèese, villain?

Serv. Soldiers, sir.

Macb. Go, prick thy face, and over-red thy fear,
Thou lily-liver'd boy! What soldiers, whey-face?

Serv. The English force, so please you.

Macb. Take thy face hence. [*Exit Serv.*]—Seyton!
　　　I'm sick at heart,
When I behold—Seyton, I say!—This push
Will chair me ever, or disseat me now.
I have liv'd long enough: my way of life
Is fall'n into the sear, the yellow leaf:
And that which should accompany old age,
As honour, love, obedience, troops of friends,
I must not look to have; but, in their stead,
Curses, not loud, but deep, mouth-honour, breath,
Which the poor heart would fain deny, and dare not.

Enter SEYTON.

Sey. What is your gracious pleasure?..

Macb. What news more?

Sey. All is confirm'd, my lord, which was reported.

Macb. I'll fight, till from my bones my flesh be
　　　hack'd.
Send out more horses, skirr the country round;
Hàng those that talk of fear.——Give me mine
　　　armour.——
How does your patient?

Doct. Not so sick, my lord,
As she is troubled with thick-coming fancies,
That keep her from her rest.

Macb. Cure her of thàt.
Canst thou not minister to a mind diseas'd;
Pluck from the memory a rooted sorrow;

Raze out the written troubles of the brain;
And, with some sweet oblivious antidote,
Cleanse the foul bosom of that perilous stuff
Which weighs upon the heàrt?

Doct. Therein the patient
Must minister to himself.

Macb. Throw physick to the dogs, I'll none of it.—
If thou couldst, doctor, purge out her disease,
I would applaud thee to the very echo.—
What rhubarb, senna, or what purgative drug,
Would scour these English hence?—Hear'st thou
    of them?

Doct. Ay, my good lord; your royal preparation
Makes us to hear.

Macb. Bring my arms after me.——
I will not be afraid of death and bane,
Till Birnam forest come to Dunsinane.   *[Exit.*

Doct. Were I from Dunsinane away and clear,
Pròfit again should hardly draw me here.   *[Exit.*

✦❦✦

Birnam Wood.

Enter, with Drum and Colours, MALCOLM, *old*
SIWARD *and his* Son, MACDUFF, MENTETH,
CATHNESS, ANGUS, *and* Soldiers, *marching.*

Malcolm.

OUSINS, I hope the days are near at hand
   That chambers will be safe.

Ment. We doubt it nothing.

Siw. What wood is this before 's?

Ment. The wood of Birnam.

Mal. Let every soldier hew him down a bough,

D

And bear't before him ; thereby shall we shadow
The numbers of our host, and make discovery
Err in report of us.

    Sold.   It shall be done.

    Siw. We learn no other, but the confident tyrant
Keeps still in Dunsinane, and will endure
Our setting down before't. The time approaches
That will with due decision make us know
What we shall say we have, and what we owe.
Thoughts speculative unsure hopes relate ;
But certain issue strokes must arbitrate.

                          [Exeunt, marching.

Dunsinane.

  Enter, with Drums and Colours, MACBETH,
       SEYTON, *and Soldiers.*

        Macbeth.

ANG out our banners, on the outward walls :
    The cry is still, *They come.* Our castle's
      strength
Will laugh a siege to scorn : here let them lie,
Till famine, and the ague, eat them up :
Were they not forc'd with those that should be ours,
We might have met them dareful, beard to beard,
And beat them backward home.—What is that
      noise ?   *[A cry within.*

    Sey. It is the cry of women, my good lord.

    Macb. I have almost forgot the taste of fears :
The time has been, my senses would have cool'd
To hear a night-shriek; I've supp'd full with horrors;
Direness, familiar to my slaught'rous thoughts,
Cannot once start me.—Wherefore was that cry ?

Sey. The queen, my lord, is deàd.

Macb. She should have died hereàfter;
There would have been a time for such a word.—
To-morrow, and to-morrow, and to-morrow
Creeps in this petty pace from day to day,
To the last syllable of recorded time;
And all our yèsterdays have lighted fools
The way to dusty death. Out, out, brief candle!
Life's but a walking shadow; a poor player,
That struts and frets his hour upon the stage,
And then is heard no more: it is a tale
Told by an idiot, full of sound and fury,
Signifying nothing.—

Enter a Messenger.

·Thou com'st to use thy tongue.

Mess.   My gracious lord,
I should report that which I say I sàw,
But know not how to do't.

Macb.   Well, say it, sir.

Mess. As I did stand my watch upon the hill,
I look'd toward Birnam; and anon, methought,
The wood began to mòve.

Macb.   Liar and slave!

Mess. Let me endure your wrath if't be not so:
Within this three mile may you sèe it coming;
I say, a moving grove.

Macb.   If thou speak'st false,
Upon the next tree shalt thou hang, alive,
Till famine cling thee: if thy speech be sooth,
I care not if thou dost for me as much.—
I pull in resolution; and begin
To doubt th' equivocation of the fiend,
That lies like truth: *Fear not, till Birnam wood*

Do come to Dunsinane;—Arm, arm, and out!—
If this, which he avouches, does appear,
There is nor flying hence, nor tarrying here.
I 'gin to be a-weary of the sun,
And wish the state o' the world were now undone.—
Ring the alarum-bell:—Blow, wind! come wrack!
At least we'll die with harness on our back.

[Exeunt.

SCENE THE LAST.

Before the Castle.

Enter, with Drums and Colours, MALCOLM, SIWARD,
MACDUFF, *&c. and their Army, with Boughs.*

Malcolm.

OW near enough; your leavy screens throw
down,
And show like those you àre:—You, worthy
uncle,
Lead our first battle: and Macduff, and we,
Shall take upon us what remains to do,
According to our order.
Siw. Fare you well.—
Do we but find the tyrant's power to-night,
Let us be beaten, if we cannot fight.
Macd. Make all our trumpets speak; give them
all breath,
Those clamorous harbingers of blood and death.

[Exeunt.

Enter MACBETH.

Macb. They have tied me to a stake; I cannot
fly,
But, bear-like, I must fight the course.—What's he,

That was not born of woman?. Such a one
Am I to fear, or nòne..

Alarums. Enter MACDUFF.

Macd. That way the noise is:—Tyrant, show thy
    face:
If thou be'st slain, and with no stroke of mine,
My wife's and children's ghosts will haunt me still.
I cannot strike at wretched kernes, whose arms
Are hìr'd to bear their staves: Or thou, Macbeth,
Or else my sword, with an unbàttered edge,
I sheathe again unheeded. Let me find him,
Fortune! And more I beg not.   [*Exit. Alarum.*

Enter MACBETH.

Macb. Why should I play the Roman fool, and die
On mine own sword? whiles I see lives, the gashes
Do better upon thèm.

Re-enter MACDUFF *through the gates.*

.*Macd.*   Turn, hell-hound, turn!
.*Macb.* Of all men else I have avoided thèe:
But get thee back, my soul is too much charg'd
With blood of thine already.
    Macd.   I've no words:
My voice is in my swòrd; thou bloodier villain
Than terms can give thee out!   [*They fight.*
    Macb.   Thou losest labour:
As easy mayst thou the intrenchant air
With thy keen sword impress, as make me bleed:
Let fall thy blade on vùlnerable crests;
I bear a charmèd life, which must not yield
To one of woman born.
    Macd.   Despair thy charm;
And let the angel, whom thou still hast serv'd,

Tell thee, Macduff was from his mother's womb
Untimely rìpp'd.

Macb. Accursèd be that tongue that tells me so,
For it hath cow'd my better part of man :
And be these juggling fiends no more believ'd,
That palter with us in a double sense ;
That keep the word of promise to our ear,
And break it to our hope.—I'll not fight with thee.

Macd. Then yield thee, coward,
And live to be the show and gaze o' the time.
We'll have thee, as our rarer monsters are,
Painted upon a pole ; and underwrit,
Here may you see the tyrant.

Macb.   I'll nòt yield,
To kiss the ground before young Malcolm's feet,
And to be baited with the rabble's curse.
Though Birnam wood be come to Dunsinane,
And thou oppos'd, be of no woman born,
Yet I will try the last : lay on, Macduff ;
And damn'd be him that first cries, *Hold, enough.*
                    [*They fight :—Macbeth is killed.*

Re-enter MALCOLM, SIWARD, ROSSE, Thanes
and Soldiers.

Macd. Hail, King ! for so thou art : Behold, where
        lies
The usurper's cursed head : the time is free.
I see thee compass'd with thy kingdom's pearl,
Whose voices I desire aloud with mine,—
Hail, king of Scotland !

All.   King of Scotland, hail !
                    [*Flourish.*

Mal. We shall not spend a large expanse of time.
Before we reckon with your several loves,

And make us even with you. Thanes and kinsmen,
Henceforth be Earls, the first that ever Scotland
In such an honour nam'd.   What's more to do,
As calling home our exil'd friends abroad,
That fled the snares of watchful tyranny;
We will perform in measure, time, and place.
So thanks to all at once, and to each one,
Whom we invite to see us crown'd at Scone.

                       [*Flourish.   Exeunt.*

9 781015 498686